PUFFI

WHIT

Born in Kasauli in 1934, Ruskin Bond grew up in Jamnagar, Dehradun, New Delhi and Simla. His first novel, *The Room on the Roof*, written when he was seventeen, received the John Llewellyn Rhys Memorial Prize in 1957. Since then he has written over 500 short stories, essays and novellas and more than forty books for children.

He received the Sahitya Akademi Award for English writing in India in 1992, the Padma Shri in 1999 and the Padma Bhushan in 2014. He lives in Landour, Mussoorie, with his extended family.

Also in Puffin by Ruskin Bond

RUSKIN BOND

White Mice

Illustrations by
Priya Kuriyan

PUFFIN BOOKS
An imprint of Penguin Random House

PUFFIN BOOKS

USA | Canada | UK | Ireland | Australia
New Zealand | India | South Africa | China | Singapore

Puffin Books is part of the Penguin Random House group of companies
whose addresses can be found at global.penguinrandomhouse.com

Published by Penguin Random House India Pvt. Ltd
4th Floor, Capital Tower 1, MG Road,
Gurugram 122 002, Haryana, India

Penguin
Random House
India

First published in Puffin Books as part of *The Parrot Who Wouldn't Talk
and Other Stories* by Penguin Books India 2008
This illustrated edition published 2018

Text copyright © Ruskin Bond 2008
Illustrations copyright © Priya Kuriyan 2018

10 9 8 7 6

ISBN 9780143428756

Typeset in Sabon LT Std
Book design and layout by Parag Chitale
Printed at Aarvee Promotions, India

www.penguin.co.in

Chapter 1

Granny should never have entrusted Uncle Ken with the job of taking me to the station and putting me on the train for Delhi. He got me to the station all right, but then proceeded to put me on the wrong train!

I was nine or ten at the time, and I'd been spending part of my winter holidays with my grandparents in Dehra. Now it was time to go back to my parents in Delhi, before joining school again.

'Just make sure that Rusty gets into the right compartment,' said Gran to her only son, Kenneth, then thirty, unmarried and unemployed. 'And make sure he has a berth to himself and a thermos of drinking water.'

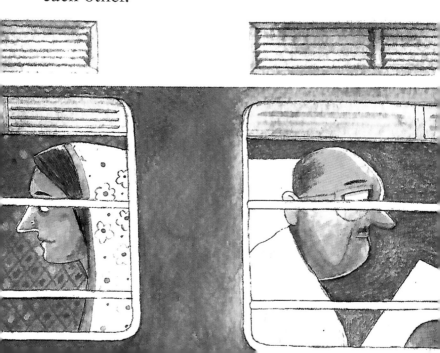

Uncle Ken carried out the instructions. He even bought me a bar of chocolate, consuming most of it himself while telling me how to pass my exams without too much study. (I'll tell you the secret some day.) The train pulled out of the station and we waved fond goodbyes to each other.

An hour and two small stations later, I discovered to my horror that I was not on the train to Delhi but on the night express to Lucknow, over 300 miles in the opposite direction!

Someone in the compartment suggested that I get down at the next station; another said it would not be wise for a small boy to get off the train at a strange place in the middle of the night. 'Wait till we get to Lucknow,' advised another passenger, 'then send a telegram to your parents.'

Chapter 2

Early next morning, the train steamed into Lucknow. One of the passengers kindly took me to the stationmaster's office.

'Mr P.K. Ghosh, Stationmaster', said the sign over his door. When my predicament had been explained to him, Mr Ghosh looked down at me through his bifocals and said, 'Yes, yes, we must send a telegram to your parents.'

'I don't have their address as yet,' I said. 'They were to meet me in Delhi. You'd better send a telegram to my grandfather in Dehra.'

'Done, done,' said Mr Ghosh, who was in the habit of repeating certain words. 'And meanwhile, I'll take you home and introduce you to my family.'

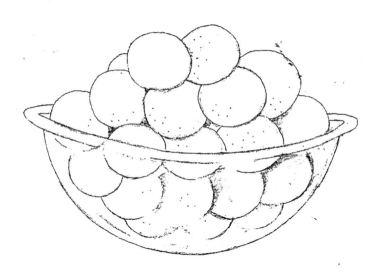

Mr Ghosh's house was just behind the station. He had his cook bring me a cup of sweet milky tea and two large rasgullas—syrupy Indian sweetmeats.

'You like rasgullas, I hope, I hope?'

'Oh yes, sir,' I said. 'Thank you very much.'

'Now let me show you my family.'

And he took me by the hand and led me to a boarded-up veranda at the back of the house. Here I was amazed to find a miniature railway—complete with a station, railway bungalows, signal boxes—and next to it, a miniature fairground, complete with swings, a roundabout and a Ferris wheel. Cavorting on the roundabout and Ferris wheel were some fifteen to twenty white mice! Another dozen or so ran in and out of tunnels and climbed aboard a toy train. Mr Ghosh pressed a button and the little train, crowded with white mice, left the station and went rattling off to the far corner of the veranda.

'My hobby for many years,' said Mr Ghosh. 'What do you think of it, think of it?'

'I like the train, sir.'

'But not the mice?'

'There are an awful lot of them, sir. They must consume a great many rasgullas!'

'No, no, I don't give them rasgullas,' snapped Mr Ghosh, a little annoyed. 'Just railway biscuits, broken up. These old station biscuits are just the thing for them. Some of our biscuits haven't been touched for years. Too hard for our teeth. Rasgullas are for you and me! Now I'll leave you here while I return to office and send a telegram to your grandfather. These newfangled telephones never work properly!'

Chapter 3

Grandfather arrived that evening, and in the meantime I helped feed the white mice railways biscuits, then watched Mr Ghosh operate the toy train. Some of the mice took the train, some played on the swings and roundabouts, while some climbed in and out of Mr Ghosh's pockets and ran up and down his uniform.

By the time Grandfather arrived, I had consumed about a dozen rasgullas and fallen asleep in a huge railway armchair in Mr Ghosh's living room.

I woke up to find the stationmaster busy showing Grandfather his little railway colony of white mice. Grandfather, being a retired railwayman, was more interested in the toy train, but he said polite things about the mice, commending their pink eyes and pretty little feet. Mr Ghosh beamed with pleasure and sent for more rasgullas.

When Grandfather and I had settled into the compartment of a normal train late that night, Mr Ghosh came to the window to say goodbye.

As the train began moving, he thrust a cardboard box into my hands and said, 'A present for you and your grandfather!'

'More rasgullas,' I thought. But when the train was under way, I lifted the lid of the box and found two white mice asleep on a bed of cotton wool.

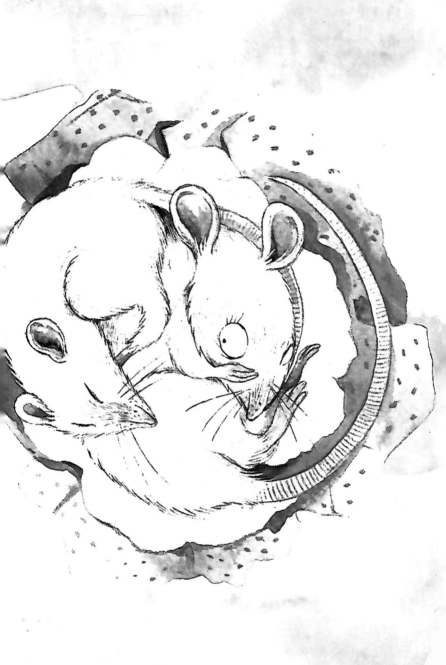

Chapter 4

Back in Dehra, I kept the white mice in their box; I had plans for them. Uncle Ken had spent most of the day skulking in the guava orchard, too embarrassed to face me. Granny had given him a good lecture on how to be a responsible adult. But I was thirsty for revenge!

After dinner, I slipped into my uncle's room and released the mice under his bed sheet.

An hour later, we all had to leap out
of our beds when Uncle Ken dashed out
of his room, screaming that something
soft and furry was running about inside
his pyjamas.

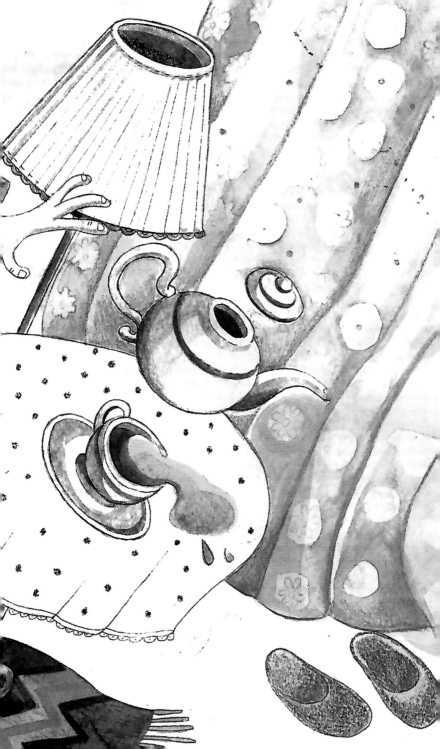

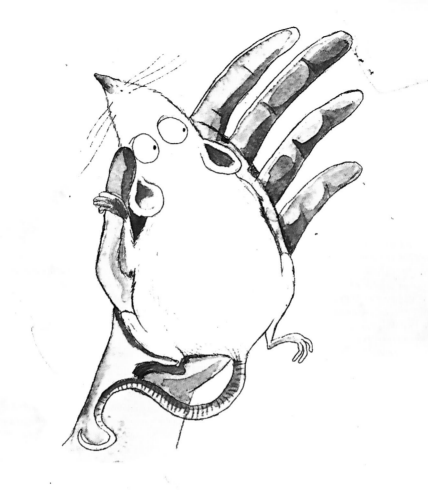

'Well, off with the pyjamas!' said
Grandfather, giving me a wink; he had
a good idea of what had happened.

After Uncle Ken had done a tap dance, one white mouse finally emerged from the pyjamas; but the other had run up the sleeve of his pyjama coat and suddenly popped out beneath my uncle's chin.

Uncle Ken grew hysterical. Convinced that his room was full of mice—pink, white and brown—he locked himself in the storeroom and slept on an old sofa.

Next day, Grandfather took me to the station and put me on the train to Delhi. It was the right train this time.

'I'll look after the white mice,' he said.

Grandfather grew quite fond of the mice and even wrote to Mr Ghosh, asking if he could spare another pair. But Mr Ghosh, he learnt later, had been transferred to another part of the country and had taken his family with him.

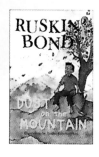

Dust on the Mountain

When Bisnu goes to Mussoorie to earn for his family, he discovers how lonely and dangerous life in a town can be for a boy. Working in the limestone quarries, with the choking dust enveloping the mountain air, he finds himself longing for his little village in the Himalayas.

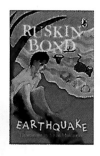

Earthquake

Everyone in the Burman household has their own ideas about what to do when there's an earthquake. But when the tremors begin and things start to quake and crumble, they are all taken by surprise. Can they survive the onslaught—twice?

Cricket for the Crocodile

Ranji's team finds an unexpected opponent—a nosy crocodile—when it plays a cricket match against the village boys. Annoyed at the swarm of boys crowding the riverbank and the alarming cricket balls plopping around his place of rest, Nakoo the crocodile decides to take his revenge.

Read More by Ruskin Bond

The Tree Lover

His mesmerizing descriptions of nature and his wonderful way with words—this is Ruskin Bond at his finest. Read on as Rusty tells the story of his grandfather's relationship with the trees around him, and how he is convinced that they love him back with as much tenderness as he showers on them.

The Day Grandfather Tickled a Tiger

When Grandfather discovers a little tiger cub on a hunting expedition, he decides to take it home. Christened Timothy, the cub grows up as any regular house pet, with a monkey and a mongrel for company. But as he grows older, Timothy starts behaving strangely, and Grandfather decides that it's time to send him away.